Say Hola to Spanish, Otra Vez

by Susan Middleton Elya • illustrated by Loretta Lopez

Lee & Low Books • New York

Text copyright © 1997 by Susan Middleton Elya
Illustrations copyright © 1997 by Loretta Lopez

LEE & LOW BOOKS, Inc., 95 Madison Avenue, New York, NY 10016

Printed in Hong Kong by South China Printing Co. (1988) Ltd.

Book Design by Christy Hale
Book Production by The Kids at Our House
Editorial consultant, Spanish language: Daniel Santacruz

The text is set in Benguiat, Frisky, La Bamba and Marguerita.
The illustrations are rendered in gouache and colored pencil on watercolor paper.

10 9 8 7 6 5 4 3 2 1
First Edition

Library of Congress Cataloging-in-Publication Data
Elya, Susan Middleton
Say hola to Spanish, otra vez/by Susan Middleton Elya; illustrated by Loretta Lopez.—1st ed.
p.   cm.
Continues: Say hola to Spanish.
Summary: Presents a humorous introduction to Spanish words through
illustrations and rhyming text.
ISBN 1-880000-59-8
1. Spanish language—Vocabulary—Juvenile literature. [1. Spanish language—Vocabulary.]
I. Lopez, Loretta, ill. II. Title.
PC4445.E492 1997
428.1—dc21   97-6851
                                                     CIP AC

To my dad for Spanish at suppertime
and to my mom for suggesting I write these books—With love, S.M.E.

For Mary, Paul, Nick, Micah (Mookie),
James, Mark and Noonie—I thank you—L.L.

Spanish is fun,
so give it a try.

¡Hola!

Hola
is hello,

adiós is good-bye.

¡Adiós!

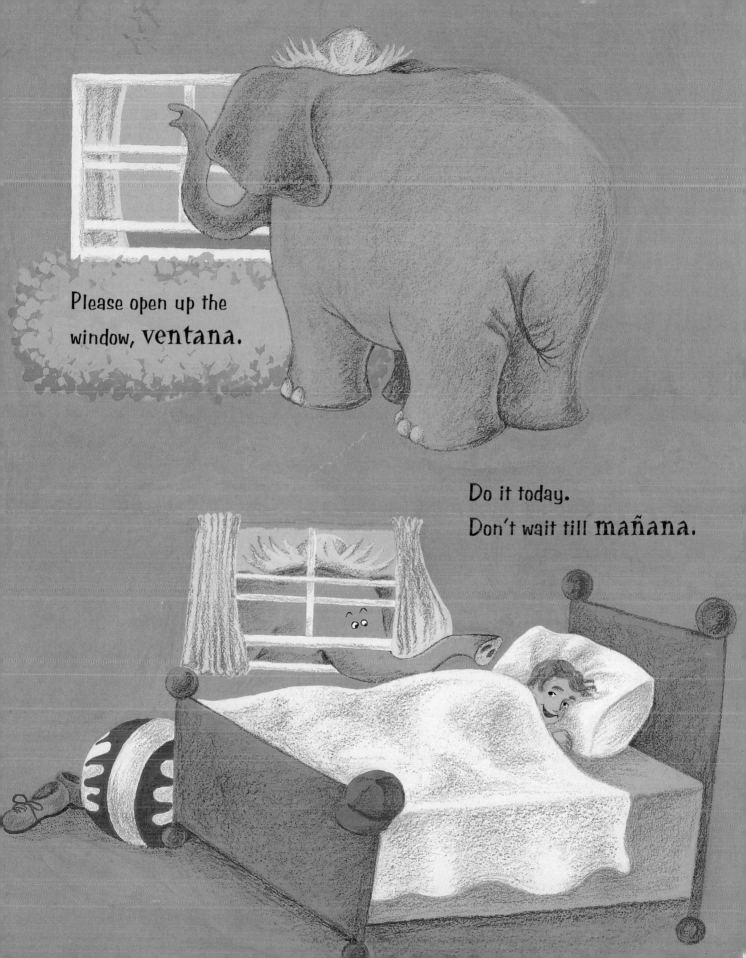

Please open up the
window, **ventana**.

Do it today.
Don't wait till **mañana**.

In the cielo, see the cometa.

The procesión has a trompeta.

Musicians are **músicos**.
Flags are **banderas**.

Please don't run when using **tijeras**.

Guitars are **guitarras**, tubas are **tubas**.

Naranjas are oranges; grapes are called **uvas**.

These are gusanos.

Guisantes
are peas.

Don't say gusanos
when dining out, please.

There goes a **tigre**.

Here comes an **OSO**.

Safer in jaulas.

Less peligroso!

Let's buy some ice cream, yummy helado.

Too much makes you gordo instead of delgado.

There goes the **mosca**

around the **abeja,**

which stings the **gallina,**

which pecks the **oveja.**

A train is a tren,

plane—avión.

A bus—autobús;

a truck—camión.

Here is a **rata**,

here's a **ratón**.

There in the water!

A big **tiburón**!

A frog is a **rana**,

a toad is a **sapo**.

Neither one's known to be very **guapo**.

Take out your **lápiz**

and some **papel.**

You'll be an **artista**
someday, I can tell.

Let's ride the **barco**   over the **mar.**

If it has a hole, we won't got too far.

Conejo is rabbit,

turtle—tortuga.

Both like to chomp on some lechuga.

Please take some fruit,

manzanas and fresas.

Or would you rather
enjoy hamburguesas?

Let's try a salad with tasty **tomate**.

After our meal, we'll drink **chocolate**.

Mountain is montaña.

Valley is valle.

Look both ways
when crossing the calle.

See the **juguetes**. A lovely **muñeca**.

Let's get some books
at the **biblioteca**.

It's getting late!
Check the **reloj**.

Rápidamente, it's time to go!

Don't forget the leche
at the mercado.

Oops! Too late!
The sign says cerrado.

Up in the sky, tonight's first **estrella**.

Look at the **luna**.
Tan grande, tan bella.

Hola is hello, adiós is good-bye.
Spanish is fun, so give it a try!

Glossary

abeja (ah-BEH-hah): bee

adiós (ah-dee-OCE): good-bye

artista (ahr-TEE-stah): artist

autobús (ow-toe-BOOCE): bus

avión (ah-vee-OHN): airplane

banderas (bahn-DEH-rahss): flags

barco (BAHR-koe): ship

biblioteca (bee-blee-oh-TEH-kah): library

calle (KAH-yeh): street

camión (kah-mee-OHN): truck

cerrado (seh-RRAH-doe): closed

chocolate (choe-koe-LAH-teh): hot chocolate

cielo (see-EH-loe): sky

cometa (koe-MEH-tah): comet

comida (koe-MEE-dah): food

conejo (koe-NEH-hoe): rabbit

cuchara (koo-CHAH-rah): spoon

delgado (del-GAH-doe): thin

estrella (es-TREH-yah): star

fresas (FREH-sahss): strawberries

gallina (gah-YEE-nah): hen

gordo (GOR-doe): fat

guapo (GWAH-poe): handsome

guisantes (ghee-SAHN-tehss): peas

guitarras (ghee-TAH-rrahs): guitars

gusanos (goo-SAH-noce): worms

hamburguesas (ahm-bur-GHEY-sahss): hamburgers

helado (eh-LAH-doe): ice cream

hola (OH-lah): hello

jaulas (HOW-lahss): cages

juguetes (hoo-GHEH-tehss): toys

lápiz (LAH-peace): pencil

leche (LEH-cheh): milk

lechuga (leh-CHOO-gah): lettuce

luna (LOO-nah): moon

mañana (mah-NYAH-nah): tomorrow

manzanas (mahn-SAH-nahss): apples

mar (MAHR): sea

mercado (mehr-KAH-doe): market

montaña (mone-TAHN-yah): mountain

mosca (MOE-skah): fly

muñeca (moo-NYEH-kah): doll

músicos (MOO-see-koce): musicians

naranjas (nah-RAHN-hahs): oranges

oso (OH-soe): bear

otra vez (OH-trah VEHSS): again

oveja (oh-VEH-hah): sheep

papel (pah-PEL): paper

peligroso (peh-lee-GROE-soe): dangerous

por favor (POR fah-VOHR): please

procesión (pro-seh-see-OHN): parade

rana (RRAH-nah): frog

rápidamente (RRAH-pee-dah-men-teh): quickly

rata (RRAH-tah): rat

ratón (rrah-TONE): mouse

reloj (rreh-LOE): clock

sapo (SAH-poe): toad

tan bella (TAHN BEH-yah): so beautiful

tan grande (TAHN GRAHN-deh): so big

tenedor (ten-eh-DOOR): fork

tiburón (tee-boo-RRONE): shark

tigre (TEE-grey): tiger

tijeras (tee-HEH-rahs): scissors

tomate (toe-MAH-teh): tomato

tortuga (tor-TOO-gah): turtle

tren (TREHN): train

trompeta (trome-PEH-tah): trumpet

tubas (TOO-bahss): tubas

uvas (OO-vahs): grapes

valle (VAH-yeh): valley

ventana (ven-TAH-nah): window